I Can Do It, Mom!

1st Day of School

Karisma L. Page

I Can Do it, Mom

Copyright © 2021 by Karisma L. Page

First Edition

Paperback ISBN: 978-1-64990-967-1

Dedication

For my bright star, Mya.

Thank you for inspiring me every day

and thank you for your focus,

determination and help

with writing this book.

Love Always

"Rise and shine, Mya."
"It's a beautiful morning today.
Let's get ready for school," said Mom.
Mom opens the curtains to let in the morning sunlight.

"I'm sooooooo sleepy.
I don't want to go to school today,"
said Mya, while rubbing her eyes and yawning loudly,
stretching her arms to the sky.

"YAWWWWWN!!!"
"Five More Minutes, please." Yawned, Mya.

"Mya, today is the first day of school!"
"Today will be a great day!" Said Mom, excitingly.

"Let me help you get out of the bed.
First, you take one leg from the bed and then the other.
Watch me!" Said Mom

THUMP!!
"YEOWWWWWW!!!" Said Mom, falling from the bed.

Mya Laughed hysterically.
"HEHE, HAHAHA, BAHAHA," as loudly as she could.

"Now It's your turn."
"Let me help you," said Mom.

"STOOOOOOOP!!!" Shouted, Mya.
"I CAN DO IT, MOM!"
"Watch me!" Said Mya, successfully not falling to the floor like Mom.

"WOOOOW!" "Great job, Mya!"
"Thank you for helping me, Mom!"
"You're welcome, dear!" Said Mom, proudly

"Time to brush your teeth."

"First you put the toothpaste on the toothbrush
and brush like this." "Let me help you!" Said Mom.

"STOOOOOOOP!!!"
Shouted, Mya
"I CAN DO IT, MOM!"

"Watch me!"
Mya puts the toothpaste on the toothbrush
and begins to brush her own teeth perfectly.

"WOOOOW!"
"Great job, Mya!"
"Thank you for helping me, Mom!"
"You're welcome, dear!" Said Mom Proudly

"Time to get dressed!"
"Let me help you with your dress," said Mom.
"First, you put the dress over your head
and put one arm in before the other.
Like this!" Mom said, excitedly.

"STOOOOOOOP!!!"
Shouted, Mya.
"I CAN DO IT, MOM!"

"You don't have to help me.
I'm a big girl now!
Look, Mom!" "TADA!"

"WOOOOW!"
"Great job, Mya!"
"You look beautiful!"
"Thank you for helping me, Mom!"
"You're welcome, dear!" Said Mom

"Breakfast is ready!"
"I'll put the jelly on the toast for you," said Mom.

"STOOOOOOOP!!!" Shouted, Mya.
"I CAN DO IT, MOM!" Said Mya.

Mya spread the jelly onto the toast all by herself.

"WOOOOW!"
"Great job!" Said Mom.

"Don't forget to put your plate in the sink."

"Table all clean!" Said Mya, proudly.

"Time for the school bus!" Said mom.
"I'm too shy," said Mya, sadly

"Let's practice together," said Mom.
"Hi, my name is Mommy,
what's your name?"

"I'm Mya." With a big smile on her face.

"Nice to meet you, Mya!"

-14-

"Do you know how to get ready for school now?" Asked Mom

"First you..."
"STOOOOOOOP," Mya shouted.
"I CAN DO IT, MOM!"

"First you get out of the bed,
then you brush your teeth,
then you get dress,
then you eat breakfast,
then you clean the table,
Annnnnnnnd, then you go to school and meet new friends!"

"Hi, my name is, Mya! What's yours?"
"PHEWWWWW!"

"That was a lot!" Said Mya
"Thank you for helping me, Mommy!"
"You're welcome, dear!" Said Mom

"There's the school bus!" Said Mom

"Let me walk you to the bus."

"STOOOOOOOP," Mya shouted.
"I CAN DO IT, MOM!"

"Watch me!"
Waving back at mom as she boards the school bus.

"Have a great first day at school!" Said Mom, proudly

"Mommy, look I did it! All by myself!!"

CPSIA information can be obtained
at www.ICGtesting.com
Printed in the USA
JSHW062237130622
27031JS00002B/6